ROOM 1

THE THANKSGIVING PLAY

TEACHER

MRS. FURBER

SHANNEN

TIM

STEPHANIE

IAN

HOLLY

SALLY

ERIC

COOPER

ALEX

BARBARA

BRETT

KIM

DANIELLE

JONATHAN

TODD

I.Q.

KYLE

1

2

I.Q. Goes to School

Mary Ann Fraser

WALKER & COMPANY
New York

First published in the United States of America in 2002 by
Walker Publishing Company, Inc.

Published simultaneously in Canada by Fitzhenry and Whiteside, Markham, Ontario L3R 4T8

For information about permission to reproduce selections from
this book, write to Permissions, Walker & Company, 435 Hudson Street, New York, New York 10014

Library of Congress Cataloging-in-Publication Data
Fraser, Mary Ann.
I.Q. goes to school / by Mary Ann Fraser.
p. cm.
Summary: Mrs. Furber brings I.Q., a rat, to be the classroom pet, but he has hopes of becoming Student of the Week.
ISBN 0-8027-8813-0 -- ISBN 0-8027-8814-9
[1. Rats--Fiction. 2. Pets--Fiction. 3. Schools--Fiction.] I. Title.
PZ7+
[E]--dc2   2001056782

The illustrations for this book were created in pencil, gouache, and pen and ink on Strathmore board.

Book design by Victoria Allen

Visit Walker & Company's Web site at www.walkerbooks.com

Printed in Hong Kong

4 6 8 10 9 7 5 3

To Todd

SEPTEMBER

I.Q. came to school on the first day.

"Children," said Mrs. Furber, the teacher, "this is I.Q. He is our class pet."

But I.Q. didn't want to be a class pet. He wanted to be a student.

Every day he watched and listened.
When Mrs. Furber read a book, I.Q.
sat quietly with his hands in his lap.
Some books made him laugh, and some
made him cry. But he loved them all.

Mrs. Furber said everyone needed
exercise. When the children went to recess,
I.Q. ran on his wheel.

Each Monday Mrs. Furber picked the Student of the Week. That student got to sit in a special chair and bring in things to share for the entire week. Mrs. Furber picked Holly's name first.

I.Q. wondered when it would be his turn to be Student of the Week.

ABCDEFG
HIJKLMNOPQR
STUVWXYZ

OCTOBER

In October the class learned the alphabet. When everyone went home I.Q. hummed the alphabet song to himself. Then he didn't feel so lonely.

During the last week of the month, the class cut out decorations for Halloween. I.Q. had trouble using scissors. He made his decorations out of tissues and string.

POOF TISSUE

NOVEMBER

In November the class learned the names of all the colors in the rainbow. I.Q. tried to color his own rainbow. The crayons were too big, so he finger painted a rainbow instead.

I.Q. had a small role in the Thanksgiving play. The night of the performance, he played his part with lots of emotion. At the end he took a big bow.

I.Q. still wondered when he would be Student of the Week.

DECEMBER

By December I.Q. could count to ten on his toes.

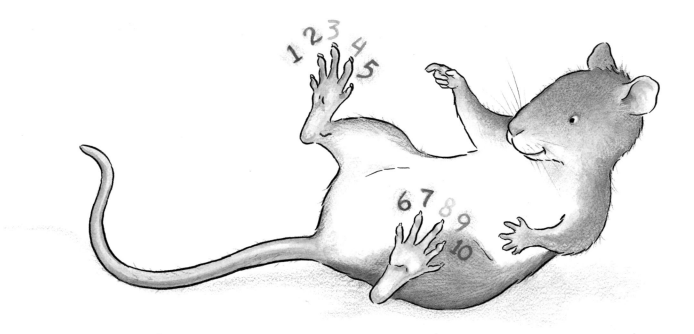

Hanukkah
Kwanzaa
Christm

Danielle, Tim, and Jonathan shared their different holiday traditions and talked about their plans for winter break. I.Q. worried that he would spend his vacation all alone at school.

But Mrs. Furber asked, "Who would like to take I.Q. home for the holidays?"

Nearly everyone raised their hands. Mrs. Furber chose Stephanie, who was sitting quietly.

I.Q.'s vacation was everything he hoped it would be.

JANUARY

After New Year's Day Stephanie returned I.Q. to the classroom. He used the treats Alex sneaked to him to learn about

more,

equal,

less,

and *zero.*

Writing was much harder to learn.
Even though he practiced holding his pencil,
his letters were very messy.

FEBRUARY

In February I.Q. made valentines for each of the other students and an extra special one for Mrs. Furber. He was afraid the children might think he was the teacher's pet, so he didn't sign his name.

I.Q. still hadn't been Student of the Week. After learning about George Washington and Abraham Lincoln, I.Q. decided he wanted to be president when he grew up. Then he could have his own special chair *and* a desk to go with it.

MARCH

In March the class studied shapes. I.Q. found more circles, squares, and rectangles in the classroom than anyone else.

SUNDAY
MONDAY
TUESDAY
WEDNESDAY
THURSDAY
FRIDAY
SATURDAY

On St. Patrick's Day the children found little green footprints all around the classroom. They thought leprechauns had come to visit. Mrs. Furber had her own suspicions.

APRIL

By midspring I.Q. could read HAT, BAT, and CAT.

For science the class planted seeds to watch them grow. The class couldn't figure out why I.Q.'s never grew.

In May the class went on a field trip to the zoo. I.Q. was not allowed to go. He thought it was because he did not have a signed permission slip.

He was sure it was his turn to be
Student of the Week, but by the end of the month
Mrs. Furber still hadn't called his name.

JUNE

There was only one more week of school left. "Maybe Mrs. Furber forgot to put my name in the Student-of-the-Week bowl," thought I.Q. He decided not to take any chances.

DEAR PARENTS,
WE WILL HAVE
A PARTY ON THE LAST
DAY OF SCHOOL.

MASTER COPY

On Monday Mrs. Furber reached into the bowl and pulled out a name. "This week's Student of the Week is . . .

I.Q.?"

Finally I.Q. had his turn to sit in the special
chair and share with the class.

On the last day of school the class had a party.
Then the children talked about their plans for summer
vacation. I.Q. was worried. He didn't have any plans.

"Where is I.Q. going for the summer?" the children asked.

Mrs. Furber smiled, "I will be working at a summer camp, and I.Q. is going to be the camp pet."

But I.Q. already knew he didn't want to be the camp pet.

He wanted to be a camper.